Aa Bb Cc Dd

Ee Ff Gg Hh Ii

Jj Kk Ll Mm Nn

Oo Pp Qq Rr Ss

Tt Uu Vv Ww

Xx Yy Zz

W9-BVJ-456

alphabet adventure

FREDERICK COUNTY PUBLIC LIBRARIES

by **AUDREY WOOD**
illustrated by **BRUCE WOOD**

THE BLUE SKY PRESS
An Imprint of Scholastic Inc. • New York

THE BLUE SKY PRESS

Text copyright © 2001 by Audrey Wood

Illustrations copyright © 2001 by Bruce Wood

All rights reserved.

No part of this publication may be reproduced, stored in a retrieval system,
or transmitted in any form or by any means, electronic, mechanical, photocopying,
recording, or otherwise, without written permission of the publisher.

For information regarding permission, please write to: Permissions Department,
Scholastic Inc., 557 Broadway, New York, New York 10012.

SCHOLASTIC, THE BLUE SKY PRESS, and associated logos are trademarks
and/or registered trademarks of Scholastic Inc.

Library of Congress catalog card number: 00-067994

ISBN 978-0-439-08069-9

27 26 25 24 23 22   15 16 17 18 19 20

Printed in China   38

First printing, August 2001

The illustrations in this book were created digitally using various
3-D modeling software packages, assisted by Adobe Photoshop.

Designed by Don Wood and Kathleen Westray

This book is dedicated to Nicoa Wood.

The little letters from Charley's Alphabet had worked hard all summer long, learning how to be a good team. At last their teacher, Capital T,

was taking them away from Alphabet Island to their first day of school. They could hardly wait. It was time for them to help a child learn his a-b-c's.

But as they were marching over a bridge, the little letter  i tripped on a bump.

"Help!" she cried, tumbling into the water below.

Working together, the letters quickly made a chain and rescued Little i.

"Good work, Charley's Alphabet!" Capital **T** said. "Now please return to your alphabet order."

The little letters were so excited that many forgot their correct places.

Some didn't face front or stand straight, and others turned upside down.

"Try again!" Capital **T** exclaimed. "And this time call out your names!"

"a-b-c-d-e-f-g-h-i-j-k-l-m-n-o-p-q-r-s-t-u-v-w-x-y-z."
They called out their names in perfect order.

n o p q r s t u v w x y z

But something was wrong with one of the letters.
What could it be?

"Little i," Capital T exclaimed. "Your dot is missing! Where is it?"

"I don't know," Little i said. "I had it this morning!"

"A little i must always have its dot," Capital T said. "We can't go to school if our i has no dot."

Capital **T** looked at the water.

"When Little **i** fell in, her dot must have popped off and floated away. Hurry! School begins soon. We must find her dot, or we'll be late."

Charley's Alphabet found a boat and hopped in. They traveled through the

canals of the island, searching for the dot. But they didn't see it anywhere.

At last they came
to a place where
the capital letters
were having a
big party.

"Maybe my dot
is at the party," Little
i said.

The little letters
searched high and
low, but they still
couldn't find the dot.

"I'm sorry," Capital **T** said. "I'm afraid Little **i**'s dot is lost forever."
Each letter had worked so hard to make Charley's Alphabet
perfect. Now no one would be going to school.
All of the little letters burst into tears.

Capital **I** stopped by to see what was the matter.

"Maybe I can help," he said. "Dots love to hide, and they're difficult to find. But I have a plan!"

Capital **I** whispered his plan to the little letters.

All of the letters, except Little i, raced down the streets of Alphabet Island,

searching for what they needed to make the plan work.

Before long, they returned with the things they had found and lined up in alphabet order.

Capital **I** spoke loudly. "Because we cannot find Little **i**'s dot, she must choose one of these things to put in its place."

Little **i** scooted
down to Little **s** and
tried on a star.
"Ouch!" she cried.
"The points on this
star are too prickly!"

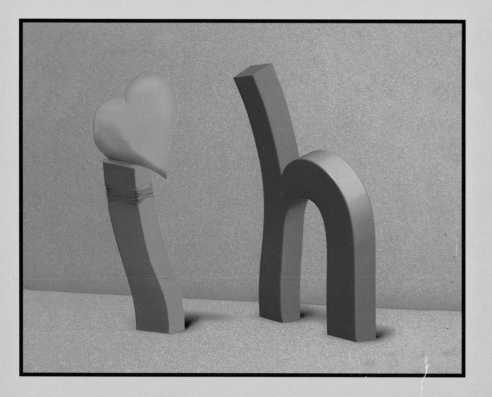

She hopped over
to Little **h** and tried
on a heart.
"This heart is too
heavy," she said. "It
makes me crumple."

She bounced
back to Little **b** and
tried on a bug.
"I can't wear this,"
she said with a
giggle. "It's too
wiggly!"

Then she noticed Little **c**.
"I think that bright red cherry
looks perfect," she said. "It's
much nicer than my dot ever
was. I don't care if my silly
dot stays on Alphabet Island
forever!"

Little **i** was about to put on
the cherry when a teeny-tiny,
weeny-whiny voice cried out . . .

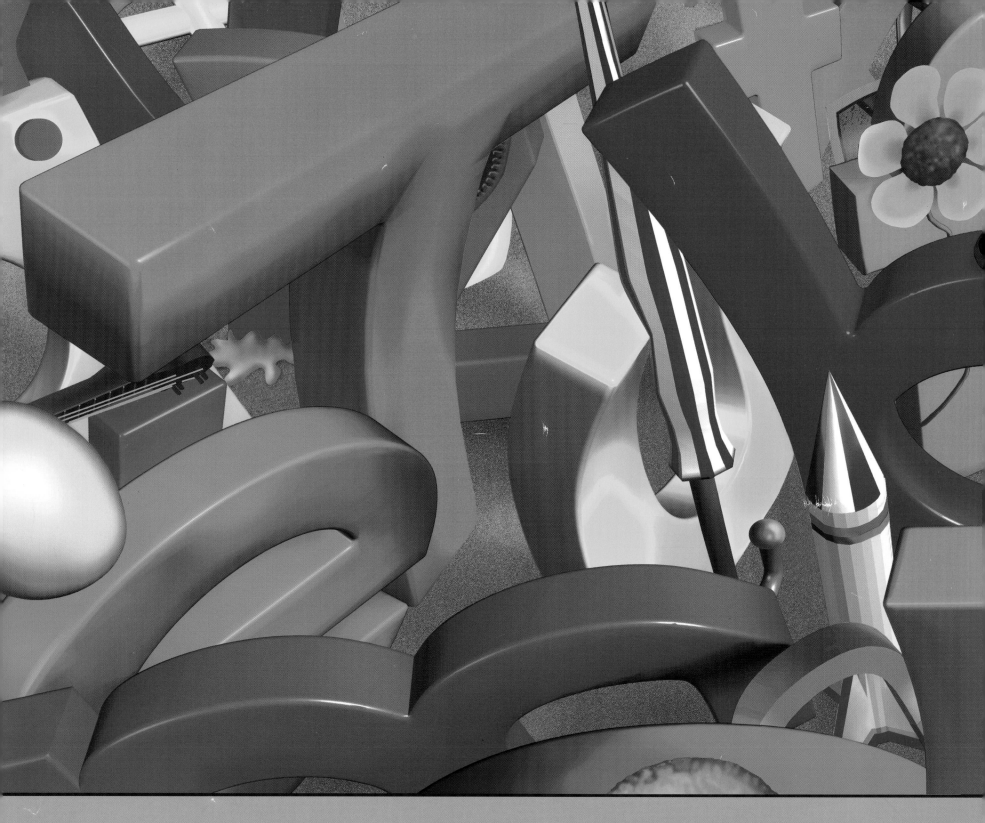

. . . "I'm not silly! You can't leave me behind." With that, Little i's dot popped out of its hiding place and jumped into its proper spot.

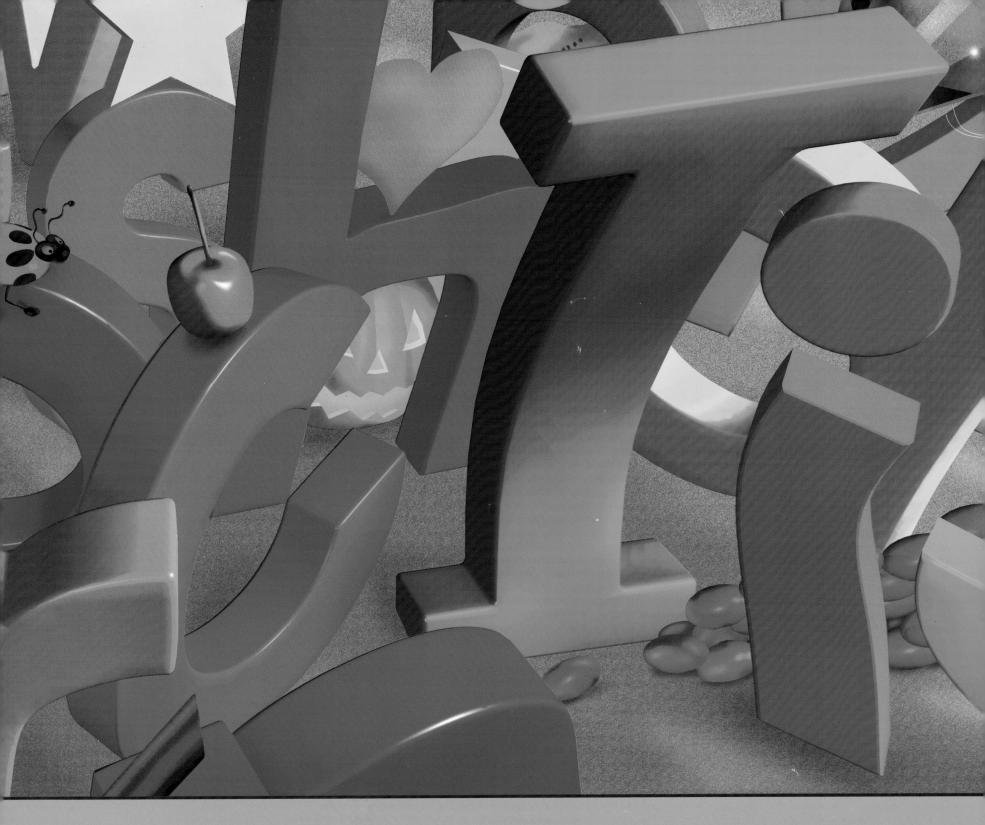

"Your dot wasn't lost at all," Capital I told them. "It was just following you around, playing hide-and-seek."

Now that they were a complete alphabet again,
all of the letters hurried to get to school on time.

One minute before the bell rang, the little letters
climbed aboard a yellow pencil and took off.

When they arrived at their school, Capital T pointed to
a boy staring at a blank piece of paper.
"It's time for you to go to work, little letters," she said.

"That boy needs your help to learn his alphabet. Can you guess his name?"
They all looked closely at the boy. Suddenly, they knew where they
belonged. The little letters were so happy, they jumped for joy . . .

. . . and made their very first word.

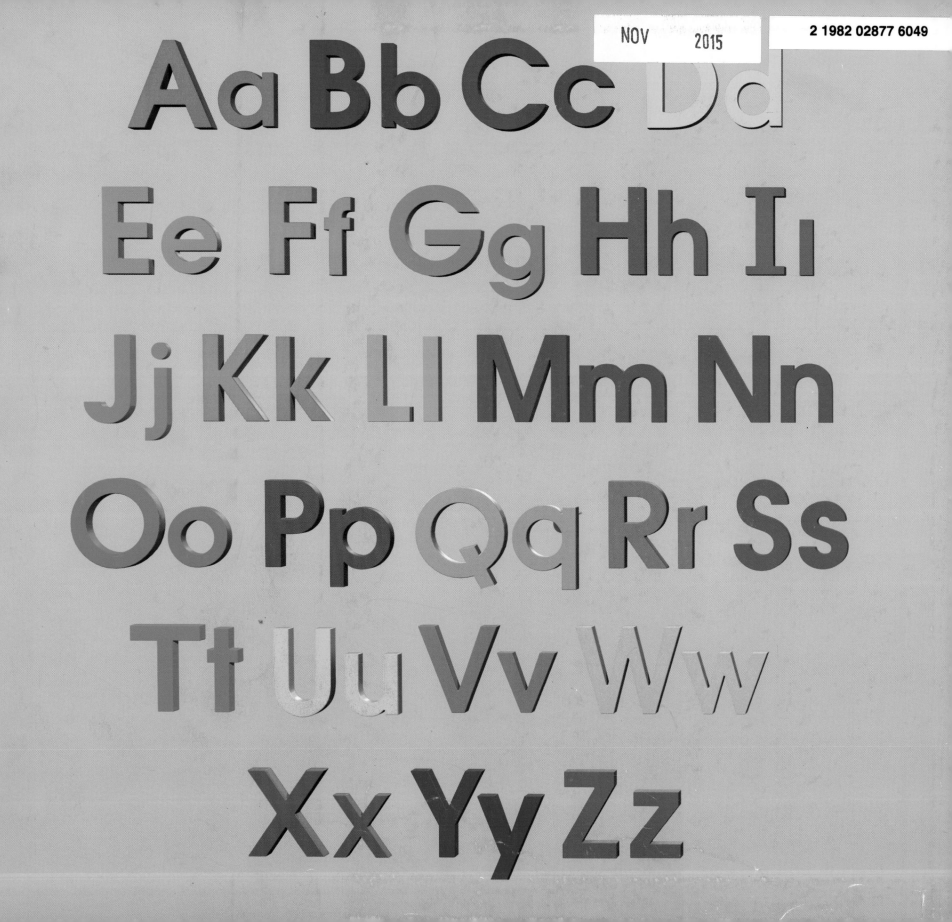

NOV 2015

2 1982 02877 6049